Blackberry Ramble

Thacher Hurd

Crown Publishers, Inc.
NEW YORK

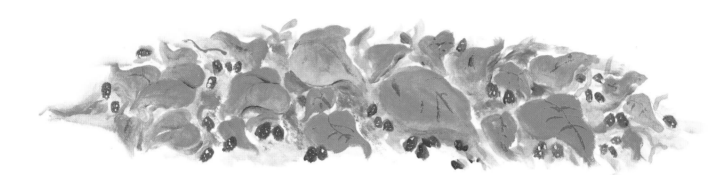

Published by Crown Publishers, Inc., 225 Park Avenue South, New York, New York 10003
CROWN is a trademark of Crown Publishers, Inc.
Manufactured in Italy

Library of Congress Cataloging-in-Publication Data
Hurd, Thacher.
Blackberry ramble/Thacher Hurd.
Summary: When spring comes to Farmer Clem's farm, Baby Mouse loves to go exploring.
[1. Mice—Fiction. 2. Spring—Fiction.] I. Title
PZ7.H9562Bl 1989
[E]—dc19
88-14188   CIP   AC
ISBN 0-517-57349-0
ISBN 0-517-57105-6 (lib. bdg.)

10   9   8   7   6   5   4   3   2   1

First Edition

For David and Brooke

When the bees sing in the flowers
and the pigs go runting in the mud,

when the radishes poke their tops through
the ground and the sun is warm once again,

then it is spring, spring on Farmer Clem's farm.
"MOOOOOOO!" called Farmer Clem's cow, Becky,
"Squawk!" said his chickens,
"Snort!" said his pigs, and

"UGH!" said Farmer Clem as he shoveled manure out of his barn. Clem, in his old overalls, was doing his spring cleaning.

In the tall grass beyond Farmer Clem's
barnyard stood a little house, the home of
Father Mouse, Mother Mouse, and Baby Mouse.

All day long the Mouse family had been
doing its spring cleaning, too.

WRRRRRRRR. Mother Mouse was vacuuming
the living room.

"AACHOO!" Father Mouse sneezed as he shook an old blanket and hung it on the line to air out.

Baby Mouse didn't say anything. She was just noodling around.

Bees buzzed in the flowers, clouds floated
by, and a far-off river laughed. All around was
the hum of everything growing, happy and
warm on a fine spring day.
Baby Mouse
ran and
jumped,

skipped,

tumbled and rolled,

into Farmer Clem's barnyard.
  She tickled the pigs,

squawked at the chickens,

and backed right into

the wrong end of Becky.

Becky's tail looked like a long rope to Baby.
Baby reached up and pulled Becky's tail as hard
as she could.

"MOOOO!" cried Becky.
She kicked up her heels and away she ran,

through the manure and across the barnyard.
    "What's gotten into that cow?" Farmer Clem
wondered. Baby Mouse held on tight.

"Whoooa, Becky!" Farmer Clem yelled. But
Becky jumped the fence, swished her tail, and:
WHOOSH! Baby Mouse went flying.

Mother and Father Mouse ran out of their house
when they heard the commotion.

"Jakers Crakers!" said Father Mouse.

"It looks like an unidentified flying object!" said Mother Mouse.

Baby flew across the garden toward Mother and Father.

THAWOP! Baby Mouse hit the blanket on the line and the blanket fell on top of her.

Baby Mouse tried to get out.
"YIKES!" said Mother Mouse. "It's a space creature."

"Baby!" cried Mother and Father Mouse.
Father Mouse hung the blanket back on the line.

By then it was late in the afternoon.

"Enough of this spring cleaning," said Mother Mouse. "Let's go for a drive."

"Yes," said Father Mouse, "let's go for a picnic supper."

Baby helped Mother and Father pack the picnic basket. Last of all they put in the blackberry pie that Mother had baked that morning.

"Mmmmmmmmm," said Baby as she smelled the pie.

The Mouse Family climbed into their old car and headed toward the big oak tree down the road.

Meanwhile, Farmer Clem was trying to catch
Becky. He was walking toward her, rattling a bucket of
corn, and saying: "C'mon, Becky, c'mon."

Since it wasn't far to the oak tree, Father Mouse
let Baby steer the car. Baby Mouse thought that
was fun.

But Baby turned the steering wheel a little too hard. "YIKES!" said Mother, and "JAKERS CRAKERS!" said Father. The car bounced off the road and through the meadow.

"WATCH OUT!" yelled Mother Mouse.
THAWHUMP! The Mouse car ran straight
into Becky.

"MOOOOO!" Becky jumped up and galumphed away. Farmer Clem just scratched his head: "What's gotten into that cow?"

Father Mouse drove the rest of the way to the picnic.

While Father and Mother laid the picnic out
under the oak tree, Baby Mouse swung on the swing.

Higher and higher went Baby on the swing,
until she almost touched the branches of the tree.
"Not too high!" said Mother Mouse.

"Yikes!" said Father Mouse.
Baby Mouse fell out of the swing,
and down,

      down,

           down,

THABLUP! into the blackberry pie.
  "MMMMMMMM," said Baby Mouse.
  "Oh, Baby!" said Mother Mouse, "now you've
had your dessert before dinner!"
  Baby Mouse smiled. It was time to eat.

After supper, Father Mouse, Mother Mouse, and
Baby played catch with their old baseball. Then
it was time to go home. They packed their picnic
basket and climbed into the car.

As the car purred along the road, Baby
heard crickets singing, bullfrogs croaking,
and pigs snoring.

Father Mouse drove past Clem's barn. Farmer
Clem was trying to push Becky into the barn:
"C'mon, Becky, c'mon!"
"MOOOOOO!" said Becky.

The sky grew orange, and a far-off river laughed.
Baby's eyelids grew heavy. Soon she was making
a sound of her own, "Zzzzzzzzzzzzzzzz," happy and warm,
dreaming of blackberry pies on a fine spring evening.